Deadly Sins: Pride

Chapter One

The Audition

Stacey was proud of what she had accomplished in her adult empire, and it was her pride which would eventually be her undoing. As with most self-made millionaires, her business started off small, but it would be tricky to see where her fortune came from hard work and dedication. She went into four years of debt on a degree and couldn't find a job to pay the bills. That's when she decided to supplement with sex toy parties. It didn't take long for the supplemental income to far exceed what she earned at her day job.

There were always problems. The supplier would have shortages. The company would raise the prices, or cut the perks associated with her earnings. Months turned into years, and her small business grew. Word of mouth spread like wildfire through the metro area, but she had to continually work harder to earn the same amount as she had in the beginning.

She took pride in her work even though most looked down their noses at her thinking she was encouraging rampant sin. She read the industry magazines arriving in the mail every month. She scoured the newsletters from the supplier detailing new products. Not a single online webinar for sex distribution sales was missed even if it meant rescheduling everything around it. There was no one more knowledgeable about what she did than her, and it reflected in her business growth. There was no question she couldn't answer, no assurance she couldn't give, and her customers were always pleased by their results.

There was a knock on her office door, and seconds later twenty year old Steve Johnson walked into her life. Stacey's poker face didn't flicker, but her eyes grinned at what she saw. The t-shirt he wore stretched tightly around his muscular chest and arms, and his athletic shorts revealed all she needed to know about what he packed below the waist.

Her new business, her new position entitled her to many perks. Judging by what was standing in front of her, Steve was set to be the biggest perk of them all.

After growing frustrated with the distribution company she worked for, she shopped around trying to find a new one, a better one. As she read through their rules and disclaimers, going over their terms with a magnifying glass, she found none of them were much better than the company she was already with, but she didn't give up. She never gave up on anything. That's how she discovered William Maddox.

He was a sex tycoon with over seventy stores in twenty-seven states. Surprisingly, he didn't have a distribution for a sex toy party operation like the rest of these companies did. The original idea was to have a meeting with him, to pitch the proposal of setting one up, with the hope of possibly even running it herself. It would be fair to the people managing their own business.

The more she researched him the more her plan evolved. He was single and had one child. He hadn't spoken to his daughter in almost fifteen years, not since the child support stopped. Seducing him to put a ring on her finger had been the hardest challenge of her life, but Stacey could accomplish anything once she set her mind to the task.

'*Seducing this young man,*' she thought, slyly unfastening the top two buttons of her blouse, '*will be like taking candy from a baby.*'

Maddox had been tight with his money. He treated his own family worse than his employees, and his contempt for his wife wasn't much better. It took years for her to get into the will. It was a harder battle than she expected. In the meantime, she implemented many changes to his company which boosted his revenue.

All of the stores had different names doing business under an umbrella corporation called Metro Media. She was the one who convinced him to make it more uniform. Before long, Secret Passions was born. She oversaw the changing of the names for all the stores, including the under new management opening day sales after renovating, if needed, and freshening up the look of the store fronts. She worked for the business, so they bent the rules a bit and brought in a lot of new customers. The sex toy party line was a major hit.

It was six years married to a man who treated everyone like scum before she reaped any real benefits. The sex party business would continue to be hers after his death. That was all he offered.

Then he became ill. It wasn't life threatening, but it was serious. Someone had to run his business if he was unable or declared incompetent while recovering.

"It's only *temporary*!" The words still haunted her. Maddox had repeated them with almost every breath for days as he signed paperwork putting her name on everything. Luckily, he was too sick to realize what all he was signing away.

By the time he died of the mystery illness which baffled doctors, Stacey was already planning her own line of sex toys, working with a company to manufacture them based on her requirements. She knew what women wanted, what they needed, and was certain the line would be successful. As always, everything she touched turned to gold.

"Have a seat," she told Steve. She slowly stood and walked to the front of her desk. "You're wanting an audition. Is that correct?"

The studio wasn't in this state, but many wannabe porn stars still called or dropped by hoping to make a buck by spreading their legs. No one did their own research anymore. Most of them were obvious drug addicts looking to score their next fix. When Steve's email arrived including full body shots, she couldn't resist the ploy. She invited him down for an audition with the prospect of being hired on the spot.

She stared at him, imagining what kind of lover he was. She hadn't lied, but the job might not be what he had expected. If he passed his so called audition, she'd find him a job somewhere in the warehouse.

The adult movie production company was the last thing Maddox worked on before he became ill. He set it up, and Stacey hadn't been too eager for the venture. It was lucrative from the start. Her husband was a businessman, first and foremost, always finding ways to keep costs down and maximizing profits. Now, she mainly stayed in her neck of the woods collecting profits while having an excuse, as well as a write off, to visit California whenever she had a whim.

"Uh, yeah." Steve looked around nervously. "I thought that's what I was doing, but..."

"But? This doesn't look like a movie set?"

He laughed nervously and rubbed his hands along his shorts.

"Exactly."

"Consider it a pre-screening then."

Steve smiled and nodded.

"So, go ahead," Stacey grinned.

He looked at her confused.

"Show me what you got." She crossed her arms over her chest and leaned against her desk.

His eyes fell to the floor then he glanced around the room until his gaze settled on the door.

"Surely, you can't be shy, not if you're looking to get into adult films."

"No, it's just that…"

"What?" Stacey was becoming bored. She pushed off the desk and headed back to her seat. It didn't appear Steve had it in him after all.

"No!" Steve blurted out and jumped off the chair. "Wait."

She stopped and slowly turned back to him. He was lifting his shirt over his head revealing a clearly defined muscle sculpture on his chest. She licked her lips and waited.

He stuck his thumbs in the waist band of his shorts and pulled them down his legs. His red boxer briefs bulged out in front of her. He was practically fully erect already. She wanted to believe it was from her, but putting on a show is a turn on for many.

"Keep going," she coaxed.

Steve removed the briefs and kicked them to the side. He stood in front of her semi-erect and completely nude except for his sneakers which had to make him feel even more awkward and out of place.

"Nice," she smiled. "There's just one thing missing."

His eyes widened, questioning what she meant with a glance. His arms kept moving in a jerking and twisting motion as he fought the urge to cover himself with his hands.

Stacey stepped toward him and took his cock in her hand. "I want to see how you look erect," she said, leaning in close until her breath landed on his earlobe. She gently stroked him until he was hard.

Leaning back, she glanced down again and was eager to experience his massive shaft personally. "Not bad," she said, expecting his ego to bruise a bit.

"Next," she began.

Steve began to reach down to pull up his clothes.

"No," she stopped him. "Not yet."

"We still have the function check to do."

His nervous glances at the office door returned. He was thinking about bolting. At the permanent age of thirty-nine, Stacey had some years on him, but she didn't look her age. Makeup and money made sure of it.

'Maybe he had a girlfriend,' she thought. *'No, not in the line of work he's considering.'* Whatever his hang up was, he wouldn't have long to make the decision to get over it or not.

Stacey turned her back to him and hiked her skirt. Her black garter and hose shown beneath, but she wasn't wearing panties. She never wore them. They were merely an obstacle to sex. She leaned over the desk and waited to see what choice Steve made.

She felt him close the distance between their bodies. His hand pressed gently against one side of her ass, lifting her into position. He aligned his cock to the entrance of her tunnel and pressed into her. Stacey adjusted her angle to accommodate him better as he began thrusting into her sopping wet labyrinth.

It was a tight fit. His girth was as impressive as his length. He began fucking her in slow, short strokes and gradually built up his speed. Stacey bucked back into him encouraging him. The moans exiting her throat were loud and would carry out into the hallway. She wanted everyone to know she was being pleasured by this hunk of a man less than half her age.

He grabbed her hips and started thrusting deep into her. There was nothing romantic about it, just pure unadulterated fucking. It was exactly the type of sex Stacey enjoyed the most.

Steve pulled out completely then pressed back into her in one long, quick stroke. He did it again and again until she reached back and held him close. She needed the orgasm now, and he was going to give it to her.

"Hard," she demanded. "Fuck me hard!"

He thrust into her as she requested. There was no finesse, just lust. It was pure animalistic fucking as he pounded his cock into her, shaking the desk and knocking everything down.

Stacey's tunnel contracted around him and began to squeeze as if trying to lock his member inside her. It began to convulse, massaging his length as her juices rained over him.

He hadn't felt a woman orgasm quite as intense as that before, and it brought him to the brink quickly. She sensed he was about to cum, so she lifted upright as she pushed him back, away from her.

Steve groaned and the shocked look on his face was almost comical, but she stifled her laugh. His cum spewed out on the desk and the floor. She frowned at the mess and straightened her skirt.

"You will clean that up," she said, nodding at the jizz sprayed about her office.

He nodded quickly and looked around for something to use.

"The bathroom is down the hall," she sighed. "Thanks for coming in, Steve. I'll let you know one way or another about the position."

She walked out of the office leaving the door wide open as he scrambled to dress himself before anyone else saw him. A wicked grin spread across her face. He was hers for the using, and she knew it.

'If it weren't for that louse whose dick I had to suck for ten years, I wouldn't be able to play like this now.' Everything about her lavish life was owed to Maddox. *'Thank God for antifreeze.'*

Chapter Two

Job Demonstration

No one else could do what she did. Most of them lacked the vision. Even more lacked the work ethic. The few who had both didn't have the guts to do what it takes.

'Worker bees. That's all they'll ever amount to being.'

Steve had settled well into his new role. He was a mixture of confused and relieved when he was offered the position of Corporate Affairs Liason. It was a generic title she had given to her toys in the past when there were no open jobs to fill. At other companies, it might be an elite spot on the team, but not at Metro Media. Here, it was simply a glorified term for a gopher.

He ran errands for the entire office. He made copies, picked things up, as well as handled some deliveries. *'But most importantly, he was my new flavor of the week as the office staff called him.'*

Stacey heard the snickers and was well aware they were gossiping about her when all conversation stopped the moment she entered the room. Let them talk. They were jealous. They envied her looks, her power, her money, and her ability to wrap any man around her little finger.

'Besides, my flavors typically last at least a month before I grow bored. This one... There's something about him which may keep my interest longer.'

The plane landed in California, and she glanced at Steve

who had dozed off during the flight. Just because he was on an airplane didn't mean he wasn't on the clock. The only reason she brought him along was to have a little fun in the air, but he annoyed her with his endless gushing about never having flown before, much less in a private plane. At the time, she didn't care when he fell asleep. At least it shut him up for a little while. It pissed her off to see him now.

"Wake up!" She yelled the words loudly while moving the arm which supported his head causing him to jerk awake rudely. "We're here," she said smiling when he looked at her.

It actually wasn't the only reason, but it was probably her favorite one. Hopefully, the flight home would be better. He was coming along to tour the studios with her. She considered making a video with him to keep, but it was too high risk. It could easily fall into the wrong hands. She would, however, enjoy testing out her most talented actors while he watched. Steve was acting like he already started catching feelings. It was time to put him in his place and see how he handled it. The one thing she couldn't stand was a jealous fuck toy ranting on and on about wanting to be her one and only.

Usually, she spent just enough time at the studios to declare it a business trip and spent the rest of the time enjoying a little rest and relaxation. This time she was mixing business with pleasure.

The car she hired was loaded and they left the airport for the hour drive. Steve's mouth began running a mile a minute as soon as the car doors closed. Stacey pulled a sleep mask from her bag and placed it over her eyes, resting her head on the side of her seat. She wasn't tired and wouldn't nap, but he didn't need to know that.

They arrived at the studios and were greeted by Mel whom she called ten minutes before, leaving him little warning the owner was on her way. He had been with the company since before Maddox bought it out. Stacey wasn't falling for this ploy. He was stopping her at the front, hoping whatever fire going on in back was put out before she got around to seeing it.

"Mel!" she cooed. "How are you?"

"Can't complain," he joked. "Who's this?" He eyed Steve approvingly probably thinking she was bringing in new talent.

"Not important," she said coldly, heading toward the hall. Mel scrambled around in front of her.

"How was your flight? Do you need anything?" He pointed to the spread laid out on a folding table. "We have a little something over here in case-"

"I'm good." Stacey side stepped around him. It must be really bad if he's trying this hard. "Steve might be hungry though." From the corner of her eye, she saw Steve veer off and pick up a plate.

She continued down the hall until she reached the end and pulled the clipboard from its slot on the wall. Running her thumb down the list, she found which room was currently scheduled for production and headed in that direction. Mel was still at her heels trying to offer any distraction he could.

The light outside the room was off indicating the cameras weren't currently rolling. It wasn't a surprise. There was obviously a problem. She opened the door and saw the entire crew sitting around talking and playing on their phones. "Why aren't you filming?"

The question was for Mel, but she said it loud enough for everyone to hear. Their heads snapped around, and they jumped to their feet once they realized who she was.

"Small hiccup," Mel began. "We had a minor script change, and we're currently waiting on another actress to arrive."

"What happened to the one you had?"

Mel sighed and lowered her eyes. "She chickened out over her anal scene."

Stacey walked past the cameras to the set. It was half a living room with a couch that had seen more ass than a toilet seat. "Where is she?"

He hesitated, but then he nodded at one of the crew who disappeared. A few minutes later, he returned with another man and a woman in tow.

She recognized both of them. Peter and Chrissy. He was one of their popular stars which only served to prove porn was a male dominated market. His looks weren't too bad, but his barely six inch, small girth cock left a lot to be desired for women. Chrissy, on the other hand, had been nothing but a string of problems and complaints since she was hired. It was time to let her go, but not today. Right now, she'd use Chrissy to show Steve how casual their relationship was in case he had any other ideas.

"What seems to be the problem?" She asked sweetly and heard a collective thud from the crew's mouths hitting the floor.

"I thought I was ready," Chrissy said, not looking directly at her.

The lack of respect infuriated her, but she had to bite her tongue. "Ready for what?"

"To do anal," she admitted.

"What is it? You're just afraid it'll hurt?" Stacey swallowed a grin. Peter's average dick couldn't hurt anyone.

Chrissy nodded. "Mel told me it only hurts for a moment,

until he's inside, but..." She shrugged. "I get myself worked up that it's really going to be painful."

Stacey sighed and pretended to pace the floor as if wondering what to do. She clicked her tongue. "How about a demonstration? To show you it's not all bad."

The young woman stared at her trying to figure out what she meant.

"Have you ever watched anal?"

She nodded again.

"Just in porn? Or in real life too?"

"Porn," Chrissy answered.

"And you know how edited that can be. I'll show you it's not so bad."

Stacey slipped her sundress off and unfastened her bra. She turned to the crew and warned them. "If any of you turn a camera on, not only will you lose your jobs, but I'll have you in court so fast your heads will spin right off your shoulders." She hadn't signed any paperwork giving them the right to record her, and they better not take advantage of opportunity.

Wearing only her heels, Stacey walked to the couch and raised an eyebrow. She knew it was cleaned regularly because she paid the bills for it. She knelt on it and leaned over the arm, lifting her ass high in the air. "What are you waiting on, Peter?"

"Oh, uh," Peter stumbled over his words. "Where's the lube?"

"Not necessary." Stacey smiled devilishly. Her ass received all the play she desired. His cock wasn't going to damage it going in dry.

Peter got in position behind her, lifting one leg for a good view like he'd been trained after years in the biz.

"That's not necessary," Stacey told him. "We're not filming. Just enjoy it."

She felt him slide between her legs, and she lowered one foot to the floor to give him more room. He reached between her legs and ran his fingers over her slit. "Peter! Just fuck my ass!"

A door closed as she ordered him to get down to it. She didn't have to turn around to know Steve had finally joined them after getting his fill to eat. *'Perfect timing.'*

Peter positioned the tip of his cock against her tight asshole. She held still, allowing him to enter her. She was completely relaxed even with the audience whose eyes were eagerly watching the owner of the company get her ass stuffed. It turned her on more.

He pushed forward, intruding into her ass. Stacey gasped while his mushroom head passed her tight outer ring. The muscles of her ass tightened around him as he progressed further. He continued until his shaft was about halfway in before pulling out and entering her again.

"Mmm, Peter," she moaned. It was for Steve's benefit, and no one else's.

His second attempt he didn't stop until his cock disappeared into her ass. Stacey leaned back into him, swallowing him inside her. He began fucking her slow and steady, but she didn't care much for that style. She liked it hard and fast.

Stacey bucked back against him, faster and faster, encouraging him to pick up the pace. Peter listened to her body loud and clear. He grabbed her hips and started fucking her hard.

She opened her mouth and let a steady stream of moans escape. Anyone who fucked her quickly learned she wasn't loud. If she made any noise during sex, it was to stroke the man's ego which she typically didn't care to do. Steve knew her to be a quiet lover, and it had to be driving him crazy with jealousy. Not only was she fucking another man in front of him, but she definitely seemed to be enjoying it, possibly more than she enjoyed sex with Steve.

It wasn't necessarily true. Steve had a delicious cock, and she found herself imagining it was his massive shaft plowing into her ass instead of Peter's.

Stacey reached between her legs and played with her clit. Peter was ramming into her ass. She could hear the occasional grunt and realized by now, he was feeling the itch. Soon, his abdominal muscles would tighten signaling to him he was close. Adult movies are editing magic. The actors can do magnificent work, but they don't always last near as long as it appears on the screen.

"Yeah, fuck me!" Stacey encouraged him. "Make me cum."

The jerking started soon after that. Peter's movements became more rigid right before he came, so Stacey increased the intensity and pressure she put on her clit to cum with him.

They collapsed over the arm of the couch with Peter on her back. He began to kiss her neck gently, and Stacey rolled her eyes. She smacked his leg lightly a couple times and told him to move.

While he continued to sprawl on the couch, catching his breath, she slipped her dress back on and picked up her bra. She approached Chrissy, and said, "See? There's really nothing to it."

"Get the girl a small butt plug for her first time and improvise," she said to Mel as she walked over to Steve.

He was fuming. If looks could kill, she and Peter would be vaporized. His hands were balled into fists at his sides, and every muscle in his body was tensed. Stacey ignored all of the signs of his anger. "Ready, sweetie?" she crooned, kissing him gently on the cheek.

Chapter Three

Finish Your Breakfast

The biggest competition to Metro Media was on the east coast. Naughty Angel made its move to an online store with easy ordering and discreet package shipment when the rest of the country was waiting for their dial up to connect. They got in early, cornered the market, and even with stiff competition, they were still holding on strong. Their internet sales were the majority of their revenue. Most of their other projects had fizzled over the years, and the ones still in operation were barely in the black.

Their online sales blew Metro Media's combined profits out of the water. For a long time, they were off Stacey's radar. They could have the internet part of sales because she dominated everything else. She didn't expect the whole world to rely so heavily on online shopping.

Secret Passions had slowly built a name for itself and was currently the second highest grossing adult company on the web. It wasn't enough. She wanted more.

Steve walked into the kitchen, rubbing the back of his head. He was groggy having just woke up.

'Must be nice to sleep the day away,' she thought, glancing at her watch. It was just after nine on a Saturday. Stacey had been up, exercised, showered and fixed herself breakfast already.

"You're up early," he said, leaning in for a kiss.

She moved away from him and turned her head, touching her fingertips to her mouth indicating he needed to brush his teeth. "Funny. I was just thinking about what a late sleeper you are."

He ignored the comment and announced he was jumping in the shower. Stacey watched him walk down the hall and contemplated joining him. She sighed as she talked herself out of it. There was work to be done.

A secret online staff had been hired by her months ago to create a smear campaign against Naughty Angel. They were a group of college students spread across the country leaving nasty reviews on their products and making comments on various posts. Some were actively bashing the company on social media. All of this while simultaneously raining accolades down upon Secret Passions. It was finally paying off. Sales had been steadily increasing. Each one of them had an affiliate link, and the customers they brought in had shot up dramatically.

It was a side project no one at the corporate offices knew about, so she only did this work while at home. Some of the staff had seen and shared the videos bad mouthing Naughty Angel with her. They just didn't realize the people on the other side of the camera were on the same payroll.

Steve sauntered back into the kitchen. She could hear him banging around the cabinets looking for something to eat. There was something unsettling about having him at the house. He wasn't the first boy toy she ever brought home, but it was rare. The others had to leave quickly. It wore on her nerves having them here, but Steve didn't bother her as much even though he was far more annoying than the rest of them combined.

"Hungry?"

His voice startled her. She hadn't heard him walk up behind her. She turned and saw him leaning against the door frame. His messy sandy blonde hair looked good on him, and he wore only a towel wrapped around his waist. She could only imagine what ideas he had for breakfast.

"I already ate," she said. Stacey turned back to her screen and locked the computer. She stood up and sat on the edge of her desk. "But if you're hungry," she said, hiking up her dress, "I might be able to find something for you."

He beamed from ear to ear and sauntered over to her. He knelt in front of her, kissing and gently biting her thighs.

Stacey spread her legs open wide and placed one foot on his shoulder. The foot still firmly placed on the floor would move up and rest on his other shoulder in time. They needed to find their balance first.

Steve explored her clit with his tongue. Stacey leaned back, arching just enough to put her box in a better position for him. He licked up and down her slit then brought his focus back to her clit. Stacey moaned in appreciation simply to encourage him to continue.

He stretched one arm up to cup her breasts. The thin material of her dress did little to reduce the feel of his hands massaging them and rolling her nipple between his fingertips. His other hand roamed between her legs until his fingers found her opening. He sucked on them one at a time before entering her. First one finger then two, and soon he had three inside her fucking her roughly.

Stacey's body welcomed the unexpected attention. Her body was overrun with sensation. In a few seconds, she was orgasming. His fingers thrust in and out faster as the waves of climax rushed over her. She dug her heels into his shoulder blades, pulling him closer until her legs defied her by shaking uncontrollably.

"My turn," Steve grinned, rocking back on his heels.

'Silly boy,' she thought. *'No one tells me what to do.'*

Stacey raised one eyebrow at him and slid off the desk. She walked a couple feet away then lowered herself to the floor, getting down on all fours. She pulled her dress up until her ass was completely uncovered, staring back at Steve. "Not until you finish your breakfast," she teased.

He walked across the floor on his knees. He grabbed her ass with both hands and pushed her cheeks up and out away from her slit. He dove face first into her thighs.

She squealed at his eagerness. The best part about having a fuck toy so young was their eagerness and their staying power. She could make breakfast last half the day if she wanted to without Steve needing a rest or issuing a single complaint. The scruff on his face tickled her inner thighs, and she made a mental note to buy razors for him to use when he stayed the night.

He buried his face deeper and took her clit between his lips. He rolled it between them before suckling on it gently. Stacey moaned again for his benefit. She had to teach him what felt great and what she didn't particularly like, and the best way to do it was with auditory feedback during the act.

Steve's tongue darted inside her. He moved it in and out quickly then slowed down and savored her taste, swirling his tongue around to graze all of the sides of her tunnel. He tried several times to move her, to adjust their position. She knew he wanted her to sit on his face, practically begged for it at times, but this position would do just fine. This act was about pleasing her, not him.

He gripped her ass with one hand and ran his other hand along her slit. His tongue flicked her clit, spinning it round in circles and massaging it between his lips.

One finger slipped inside her. He crooked it gently and found her g-spot just like she'd taught him. *'Good boy,'* she thought.

Stacey bucked back into his face to show her appreciation for the technique. She grinded her ass into him, begging for more.

Another finger slid into her labyrinth. He didn't take his mouth away from her clit while he fucked her with his fingers. He caressed her side, moving his hand from her ass to glide underneath her and massage her breasts, first one than the other.

His third finger made its way inside her. She was getting close. She leaned into him, lifting her ass and grinding into his hand. Moans of excitement slipped from her mouth, growing in intensity and pitch. It made her feel like she was howling like a dog, but it was to let him know she was about to cum. "I'm almost there," she told him.

He lifted his head from her mound, and she sensed he was moving into position to fuck her. That's not what she had asked him to do. *'What the hell? Why would he change positions now?'*

Stacey shot forward and rolled on her back, crossing her legs. "I told you to lick your plate clean."

"I did," he smiled, leaning down over her.

"You missed a spot." She looked him in the eye, challenging him and spread her legs apart again. She placed both hands on his shoulders, pushing him back down where he belonged.

Steve buried his face again, and she grabbed hold of his head, holding him in place. It was growing tiresome having to repeatedly coax him down to finish the business he started.

She thrust into him, fucking his face. He tried to pull back, but she wasn't letting him come up for air until she came again. He wrapped his arms around her legs and rubbed her clit with his thumb.

"That's it," she told him. "Right there. Don't stop. Don't change position. Don't move a muscle." The words spat from her mouth. If he ruined her orgasm again, she'd kick him out of her house with only the towel to cover himself.

Stacey's entire body tensed up. Her climax released, and she buried his face into her, grinding into him harder and slower as she rode it out. Her juices flowed from her tunnel and covered his face in her sticky wet cum. The walls of her labyrinth constricted and tried to find something to cling to. When nothing was found inside her, it convulsed harder searching in vain.

'Damn!' She hadn't realized how much she needed that this morning. Steve was proving useful for something. It had only taken weeks to learn what it was.

As soon as her orgasm finished, she got to her feet and smoothed out her dress. Her phone had been vibrating for several minutes. Something important was going on, and she picked it up, checking her texts.

"Your turn," Steve said in a sing song voice.

From the corner of her eye, she saw him remove the towel and drop it on the floor next to him.

Stacey held a finger out to him, telling him to wait. There was a series of messages and missed calls from one of the college kids she'd hired to go after Naughty Angel. Trish was a science geek and had tested a variety of their dildos. The rubber to silicone ratio was drastically disproportioned, and the toys shouldn't be marketed as silicone with that mixture. It made them much lower quality than the price tag and advertising suggested.

This was going to be huge. There would be demands for refunds. They'd have to give out discounts and other enticements like crazy if they wanted a chance of keeping any of their customers. This was a punch that would keep on giving. Not only were they taking advantage of customers by charging for something they clearly weren't delivering, but it meant the toys wore out faster as well. Customers would have to purchase another toy much faster from Naughty Angel than they would if they had shopped at another company. *'Like Secret Passions for example.'*

It was music to her ears. Nothing could have made her day better. She finally had the smoking gun she needed. Naughty Angel was going to be hit hard when word got out.

"Stace," he called out.

'God, I hate it when he calls me that.' She turned to him to see what he wanted.

"It's your turn," he said again. He gently gripped the base of his hard cock with one hand and winked at her.

"I told you," she said, grabbing a few things off her desk. "I already ate." Stacey ran upstairs to clean up and think about how to proceed with this new information, leaving a very disappointed and frustrated Steve on her office floor.

Chapter Four

The Lounge

They couldn't last a day without her. It wasn't conceit talking. Every time she attempted to go on vacation, the office called her a dozen times a day. "So sorry to bother you, but..."

Their incompetence never failed to astound her. Stacey would give anything to go just one day without someone asking for her approval, her advice or acknowledgement on something. She's always known no one could do what she is capable of doing, and it shows.

Steve had gone home for the weekend. His youth was what attracted her to him. It was his youth which held the handsome looks she wanted on her arm, the strength to make her feel protected, and the endurance to satisfy her. It was also his youth which irritated her.

It was a sign of his immaturity. He got his first full paycheck and decided to drive two hours to visit mommy. Real adults only went back home when absolutely necessary: funerals and weddings. If there was a way to get out of going to them, they'd jump at that chance too.

The last couple days before he left there was no time for any of their regular nightly activities. She had been booked solid with business meetings. There were details to iron out over a couple new toys in her product line. The studio in California needed help navigating the new laws and codes regarding filming adult content. It was nothing she couldn't handle, but it made for long days which left her exhausted.

That's why she was on the prowl tonight. She stepped from the car, handing the keys to the valet. Her phone was switched to silent, and she tucked it away in her handbag. There was no emergency which couldn't wait until the morning. Stacey walked into the restaurant and was greeted by the hostess.

"Good evening. Do you have a reservation?" The young blonde eyed her questioningly. Coming in alone, she was either meeting someone in particular in the dining room or hoping to meet any someone in the lounge downstairs.

"Yes, for *the* hunter," Stacey told her. A new name was issued every week. It sometimes happened more often if there was an unruly patron. Only the elite, the best looking, the most discreet received the updated changes regularly. Everyone else waited on standby in the hopes business was slow.

The hostess tried to hide her smirk, but failed. "Right this way," she said, taking a drink menu from below the podium.

Stacey followed her down the hallway along the side of the dining room. Openings in the wall allowed her and the guests to spy each other as she passed. A set of glass double doors at the end of the hall were opened by the hostess' key card. "Enjoy," she smiled carefully handing her the menu.

It made her wonder what the diners thought, seeing people escorted to the back. If it was a private room, why was it never available to book for parties? She'd never been in that position to wonder how the other half were living.

Once through the doors, she opened the menu and took out the round, thin card hidden inside. She tossed the menu toward the shelf on the wall, but it missed and landed on the floor. She continued walking. It wasn't her job to straighten anything.

A few feet down was an elevator, and she pressed the call button. The doors opened immediately. One floor below, the doors opened again, and a bouncer appeared.

Stacey handed him the disc and waited.

He entered some information into his tablet and said, "Number forty-seven. You just made it."

'I dare you or anyone to deny me entrance,' she grinned.

The bouncer pulled a card attached to a lanyard and swiped it on the side of the tablet then held out his hand.

She opened her purse and gave him a credit card which he swiped to connect to the account. It was a pointless exercise. Women didn't pay a cover, and she certainly wasn't shelling out her own dough for any drinks. Still, it was a mandatory practice.

When he finished, he took her purse from her and stored it in the safe in the coat room. He placed the lanyard around her neck and gruffly told her, "Have a good time."

Stacey walked through the doors of the lounge. The layout was in need of a remodel, but it served its purpose. There were people everywhere, grouped together and making out in the open. It didn't take long to find what she wanted. A man sat on a sofa with two women lavishing his body with their mouths. He was gorgeous, tan, and looked to be in his early thirties.

She walked directly to him, ignoring anyone who tried to approach her along the way. "You," she said, motioning with her finger for him to come. "Do you have friends?"

The man stood up, sliding one of the women off his lap who pouted and glared at her. He waved and snapped his fingers to get the attention of two other guys before approaching her.

"Pick a room," she ordered.

He grinned and led the way to a private room on the side with a red vacant light above the door. Stacey yelled an order to a passing waitress along the way. Once they arrived at the private room, he stopped and waited.

Stacey gave him a look. If he thought she was paying for it, he needed to go back to the double mint twins on the cum stained sofa.

The man looked hesitant, but swiped the card around his neck, and the door unlocked. They walked inside, and he held it open for his two buddies. "I'm Tyson," he said.

"I don't care," she replied coolly. Stacey walked to the far side of the room, lifted her leg onto the sofa pressed against the wall, and faced the door. When all three were present, and the door had closed behind them, she asked, "Who's first?"

The man from the lounge didn't answer. He walked up and forced her to squat on her haunches, reaching into his back pocket for a coarse linen cloth. Stacey squatted, remaining perfectly still while he wrapped the blindfold around her head, tying it securely. The knot pressed into her hair.

He pulled her to her feet and lifted her dress over her head. Soon after, her strapless bra fell to the floor revealing her nude body. Panties only ever got in the way.

One man fondled her breasts while another pulled her arms back and bent her over. Hands caressed all over her body. She couldn't tell one man from the next. One set of hands behind her, one on her breasts, and one invading her pussy from below.

There was a quick knock at the door, and the hands exploring her outer folds disappeared. She could hear voices as they placed a drink order and paid for the one the waitress brought for her.

Then there was silence. A foot nudged her legs apart, and she could feel the tip of a cock lining up to penetrate her. He forced forward and fucked her from behind. The vent kicked on and cool air blew over her naked back while his fingers dug into her hips.

Another set of hands pushed her head down. A voice ordered her to open her mouth, and she obeyed. The salty warm shaft barreled into her mouth, gagging at the back of her throat while the hands held her head in place, moving her head back and forth before letting up, letting her gasp in a breath of air. Then he repeated it again and again.

The man behind her slid in and out. His muscular legs pressing against her inner thighs, forcing them open wider. He plowed into her hard, slapping against her ass, and she could feel the heat rising on her butt cheeks as they reddened. If her mouth were free, she'd moan willingly.

He pulled out and pushed her forward until she hit the edge of the sofa. He bent her over the arm while one of the men laid underneath her, taking her nipples between his teeth, biting them till she cried out. He stopped, massaged them roughly with both hands then bit them again.

A different cock forced its way in her labyrinth from behind. This one was shorter, thicker. Stacey didn't know which man was where on her body anymore. The thought made her legs tremble, and she began to cum.

"Fucking slut," she heard the man fucking her say.

'That's right. I'm a slut, but I'm your fucking slut.'

His hands pushed her to the side again. They led her to the front of the sofa where another set of hands pulled her onto someone's lap backward. She straddled the cock being presented, taking it into her tunnel in one long stroke. The man gripped her sides and guided her up and down on his member.

Another cock smacked against her cheek. She reached up, blindly feeling for it until she made contact and leaned in to suck it.

"Don't forget me." It was another voice. Another cock presented to her face. She took turns, sucking one while stroking the other. She switched back and forth, taking care to not give one more attention over the other. The whole time the dick below thrust up into her. She rocked back and forth until she came again.

The man fucking her pushed her over and shoved his dick in her mouth. "Suck it clean, you dirty whore!"

He thrust his rigid cock deep inside her gagging throat. There were still two others in the room, watching, maybe waiting for their turn. His cock was the only one at the moment, and she sucked it hard, playing with his balls, until he shot his load in her mouth.

"I'm out," he told his friends.

The sound of a zipper could be heard, and Stacey sat up, panting, wondering if it was over already. Then she heard the voice of the waitress and realized why she hadn't been receiving as much attention.

"Thirsty?"

Stacey shook her head.

The hands were back. Four of them. They moved her until she was on her knees in front of the sofa. She opened her mouth expecting to suck them all dry.

"Not so fast." One of the men chuckled.

She felt three fingers penetrate her tunnel and lift her until she was bent over the sofa.

"That's more like it."

One of the men positioned himself between her legs, spreading them as wide as he could. He bent over and whispered in her ear, "I'm not gonna lie to you. This is going to hurt."

"Yes!" Stacey couldn't help herself. "Fuck my ass!"

Both men laughed.

"Oh, you want it?" The man behind her asked.

She buried her face down, poking her ass up as high as she could. "Yes, please."

"Be careful what you wish for." He pressed his tip against her tight asshole and pressed forward, not stopping until his full length was inside her. He grabbed a handful of hair and wrapped it around his wrist, pulling it hard, yanking her head back. He thrust deep into her ass, fucking her without mercy until he pulled out, and shot his load over her back.

"All yours," the voice said.

"How do you want it?" The third man asked.

Stacey turned toward his voice. "Dealer's choice."

"You might regret that," he teased.

'Not a chance.' This is exactly how she liked it. Dirty. Nasty. Down to business. No foreplay needed. The best part was they didn't know her here. There was no awkward morning after or phone calls to avoid.

It was the larger cock, the first one to violate her cunt. He thrust several long strokes into her then pulled out and slammed his full shaft into her ass. He kept a tight grip on her shoulders, not allowing her to move, switching between her ass and pussy. Several slow strokes into her wet tunnel then one quick and hard into her ass.

Stacey had just picked up the rhythm when he changed it up. He plowed into her ass and stayed, fucking into her like a jackhammer. A long shrill moan flew from her lips and just as she started to cum, he pulled out and came on her face.

He ripped the blindfold off and left the room, zipping his pants as he went. Stacey lay over the sofa, gasping for breath, feeling used and worthless. *'God, I love this place.'*

Chapter Five

Second Chances

It had been a long week putting in extra hours because almost all of her staff were incompetent. In her experience, none of them were capable of doing the work she could, so changes were made.

When she first took over the company, she paid her employees well, gave them an amazing benefit package, time off with pay, the whole nine yards. What did she get in return? Deadlines were almost never met. The completed work was shoddy at best. Call offs happened far too regularly. However, they had no problem depleting the free resources she provided. Coffee supplies and other items like bottled water and snacks had to be replaced far too often. It didn't take a degree in accounting to figure out the deadbeats working for her were taking the crap home to help support their own kitchens.

Replacing the employees didn't change anything either. Everyone she hired turned out the same regardless of their resume or past accomplishments. It didn't take long for her to give up.

Stacey fired the whole lot of the office staff and started with a clean slate. She got rid of the office freebies. There was a coffee pot, but it was bring your own or let it collect dust. The benefits were cut and cost of insurance per employee was increased. Paid time off wasn't accrued by hours worked, but given as a lump sum after a year employment. The starting pay was reduced to minimum wage.

There was something she didn't advertise. Any employee who made it one year without missing more than three days got it all back. Everything she used to offer her workers, except for free snacks, was handed over to them. By now, they figured it out because several of them had made it. That didn't change how hard it was for someone to show a little work ethic to reap the rewards. Three call offs in a year without proof of death in the family or illness meant immediate termination.

Single moms were the best, but it was a crap shoot. Some called in every other day because one of their crotch goblins was sick, but some of them would work until noon on the day of their funeral because they had bills that weren't going to pay themselves. The problem was most single moms didn't want the stigma of working for an adult company.

Of the twelve bodies floating around outside her office door, there were three women worth what she paid them. The rest were good for little more than making copies, filing and answering the phones. Any real work they did had to be checked.

It had been over a week since the last firing, and as terrible as that girl Jessie was, the work was piling up without a replacement hired yet. Stacey was worn out, and Steve had once again gone home to visit his mommy which meant her stress relief would have to wait. However, there is a light at the end of every dark tunnel.

Jessie had called a couple times, begging for her job back which overly annoyed Stacey. Yes, times were bad all around. Yes, good jobs were hard to find. That's why it's not smart to fuck things up in the first place.

She kept carrying on about how all her call offs were verified. Whatever that means. This last time was because her grandma had a heart attack and was in the hospital which she could prove.

'Like that makes one bit of difference. Grandma will still be there when you clock out. If not, visit her at home or use the bereavement pay I still offer everyone.'

Stacey didn't understand a person's over connection to families at all. The one thing she did comprehend fully was not waiting until threat of death to be there. It wasn't something she would do. Her family hadn't ever done a damn thing for her. For those who claimed to care about their people, they mainly showed up when the end was near.

When Jessie finally gave up, her husband Brett took over. Stacey was embarrassed for the poor girl. It must be extremely humiliating to have someone else call to try to get your job back. Stacey ignored all of his calls until she stalked Jessie's social media. It was standard when someone was fired. She liked to see if the former employee was bad mouthing the company.

That's when she saw Brett's picture. And, damn! Jessie was a pretty girl, but she wasn't eye candy like Brett on her arm level of pretty. This changed everything. With Steve out of town, there might be something Brett could do to help his wife if he was willing. She scheduled the meeting for Friday after hours, claiming she had a late meeting. The only thing on her agenda was getting work from the week caught up and would be in need of something to relax her afterward.

She buzzed him in the outside door when he arrived. The email she sent had given him instructions on how to get to her office. It was pretty easy to find. She had explained in her message depending on when the staff left, there may not be anyone to show him up. It wasn't a complete lie. Actually, it was more like a complete truth. She simply left out the part where she knew the staff would've gone home hours earlier because she didn't allow overtime. Not being a liar was one of the many things she boasted about herself.

A few minutes later, there was a brief knock on the door. "Come in," Stacey called out.

Brett walked into the office and stumbled over his words when he saw her. There was no one more sure of her beauty than she was, but she imagined her face wasn't the only thing to have him tongue tied.

Stacey sat behind the desk completely nude. Her breasts were still perky thanks to a very talented doctor, and they greeted Brett as warmly as her smile did.

He had that deer in headlights look about him. His feet were nailed to the floor. His eyes glued to her supple breasts. In a few seconds, he'd bolt.

"I'm so sorry," she cried, pretending to be humiliated. "I forgot about our meeting." Stacey jumped up and scrambled to pick up the robe laying over her desk, wrapping it around her quickly. "I thought you were Steve."

Brett's eyes darted away, and he began making his apologies. He wasn't going to leave now. Men were so easy. Getting them to do what she wanted was like child's play. It would, and normally did, bore her, but tonight wasn't about Brett. It was about Jessie and getting her to leave the company alone. If she needed the job, she should've shown up to work. It's really that simple.

He had been shocked when he walked through the door of course. Sure, he loved his wife and would never cheat on her, but he couldn't look away either because Stacey was desirable.

It made him uncomfortable though until he thought it was a mistake, an accident on her part. Now, he would sit there, trying to win his wife's job back, but wouldn't be able to get the image of Stacey's naked body out of his mind.

Stacey listened to him as he made an appeal for his wife. Well, that was a bit of a stretch. She allowed him to ramble on about his wife's strengths and assets. All of which were nothing she cared to hear. As he spoke, she made a mental list of things she needed to do when she got home to prepare for her busy day tomorrow. Occasionally, she added an encouraging, "Yes, I see." Or, "Uh-huh." Once when he was losing speed, she added a well-timed, "You make a valid point, but," then allowed him to carry on with renewed gusto, thinking he was making progress.

Near the end, she interrupted him for a phone call. She had called herself with her business cell under the desk and pretended it was Steve canceling their plans. With fake tears shining in her eyes and a crack in her voice, she ended the meeting, telling Brett he'd given her plenty to think about. Men can't resist a crying woman. It either drives them up a wall or makes them want to hug the pain away. It was a risk, but she had Brett pegged as the latter. When she stood to show him out, her robe may had accidentally slipped off. It may have had help. Brett never asked, but he did savor the chance for a second look.

When he pulled on his jeans to readjust for his erection, she smiled. It was in the bag. "There might be something we could work out," she said with a wink. "I'd love to give Jessie a second chance if we could come to some sort of agreement."

It took very little convincing after that. Brett fucked her over the desk. She rode him on one of the chairs, and he fucked her so hard on the floor she was going to have rug burn for weeks.

The stamina on this one was unreal. It felt so good making Jessie's husband hers. Maybe she'd think twice about begging next time. Be careful what you wish for.

Of course, he was worried about his wife finding out, and Stacey promised him she wouldn't breathe a word about their sleeping together, and she kept her word. She never told Jessie the two of them fucked. "However, if you ever find your needs aren't being met in the future, I'd love to help you out," she teased.

Brett's eyes were filled with regret when he left. It wasn't from sleeping with her. No one ever wished they hadn't taken a drive through her fun tunnel afterward. It was purely from cheating on his wife. If he didn't have that ring on his finger, he'd be back for more by the end of the weekend. She'd bet money on it, and she wasn't the gambling type.

"Tell her to be here Monday," Stacey said, closing the office door behind him. "The usual time."

Once she heard the elevator doors close as he left, she went back to her desk and searched the employee files on the computer for Jessie's number. Two rings, and she answered.

"Hello?"

"Hello, Jessica. It's Stacey. Stacey Maddox." She used that name because it was associated with the porn empire her late husband had built. It was recognizable in these circles. Everything was actually in her maiden name. She had never changed it when they got hitched.

"Hi," Jessie said. There was an uncertainty in her voice.

"I was calling because I just met with your husband, wonderful man."

"My husband?" It wasn't surprise in her voice. He had told

her about the meeting. It sounded more like fear.

"Yes, and he convinced me to give you a second chance. We'll see you Monday morning."

"Really?" Jessie practically screamed. "Thank you so much. I promise I won't let you down."

Stacey rolled her eyes. *Funny. Why didn't you do that in the first place?'*

"It will be on a probationary status, of course," Stacey explained.

"Yeah, I understand." Jessie was too happy, too eager. It turned Stacey's stomach.

"By the way, your husband's tattoo is amazing. Where do the two of you go to get your ink done?"

"His tattoo?" Jessie's voice fell. All traces of excitement were gone. Stacey could've hung up then, and she would've known the truth.

"Yes, the snake wrapping around his leg. It's beautiful artwork, really."

"How do you know about that tattoo?" The words rasped out of Jessie's mouth slowly. Stacey imagined her hand to her chest, tears rolling down her cheeks while she struggled to remain calm and keep her composure until after the phone call was over.

Stacey smirked and spoke carefully. "Because I traced it with my tongue before I sucked his hard cock into my mouth."

The line went dead, and Stacey laughed as she cradled the phone. Jessie didn't show up for work on Monday or call about the job again. *'I guess she doesn't want to work too badly after all.'*

Chapter Six

Intercom

Jessie's replacement had Stacey quickly wishing she had never slept with Brett. No, she never regretted a conquest. If anything, she shouldn't have rubbed it into Jessie's face.

Ashley was young, slim and gorgeous. She won the genetic lottery. Her father was Italian, and she was raised by her mother's family in Barbados. They moved to the states before she was a teenager, but enough of her accent remained to make her intriguing without even seeing her face. She was confident and kind. The woman dressed and dolled herself up like every day could be the day a talent scout discovered her making her the next A-list celebrity. Everyone flocked to her and fawned over her.

This wasn't the first pretty face to grace her staff. There had been dozens over the years. Some were still in the blissful honeymoon phase of being happily married. Others might have been graced with looks, but lacked anything else. There had been one beauty Stacey still expected to see on a late news report one day. The girl was pure evil. None of them could hold a candle to Ashley.

It wouldn't have bothered Stacey. She had two things this girl didn't. The first was her exceptional abilities in bed. She fucked like a queen and could drain any man's nuts with her mouth in under a minute. Most importantly, she had money and a lot of it. Anyone who says they're not attracted to money or would never date someone because of their money is a liar.

The problem began when Steve noticed the new girl. He's a hot blooded man. A beautiful woman is going to catch his eye. It's when he started paying a little bit too much attention Stacey became irritated.

Every other time she needed him he was on an errand for the office. He might be picking up their lunch order at a place without a delivery option. Suddenly he was a handyman fixing every loose hinge and squeaky drawer in the building. The staff learned if Ashley asked him to do it, he couldn't refuse. They took advantage of it.

For the first couple weeks, they snickered behind his back. He was the butt of their jokes the way he fell over himself to do anything she wanted. It made him less attractive to Stacey, and she went on the prowl more instead of playing with her toy. If it had continued, she'd have tossed him and found someone new. It wouldn't be long until she live with lifelong regret of not doing exactly that, but her pride insisted on teaching Ashley a lesson instead.

Then she noticed the whispers. Whenever she came in the room, their chatter quieted. She was used to that. They were intimidated by her and should be. One day she heard Steve's name mentioned in their quiet huddles, so she paid attention.

It seems dear little Ashley had a crush. She wanted to ask him out, but was afraid of Stacey firing her.

'They'd both be out on their asses if he did me like that,' she fumed. *'I give you a job, and this is that thanks I get.'*

She wanted to fire her on the spot, but decided to have a little fun first. It had been close to an hour after she called him when Steve opened the door to her office.

"About time," Stacey spat.

"Sorry. I was in the middle of something then the warehouse needed me."

Stacey's lips pursed together in a straight line. "Who pays you?"

He shifted his weight nervously. "You do."

"Don't make me wait again. What's that?" Stacey pointed to the clipboard in his hands.

"Uh," Steve stammered, looking at the papers on it.

They should be naked by now. Stacey's irritation was flaming.

"The warehouse needs you to sign these. Work orders and invoices, I think."

Stacey rolled her eyes and reached for the clipboard. The top paper was from the landscaping company who handled the property. She scribbled her name across all the forms on the clipboard and handed it back to Steve.

"You have two minutes."

"For what?"

"To run that clipboard to the warehouse and get back here. If you make it, you can have me. If not, you can watch me fuck someone else. Go!" She looked at her watch.

Steve's mouth fell open. "There's no way. It's downstairs on the other side of the building."

"One minute, fifty seconds." Her eyes were fixed to her wrist.

He ran from her office, and she laughed, kicking off her heels. He'd make it. One way or another, he wouldn't let her down when her pussy was at stake.

She was still unbuttoning her blouse when he flew through

the door panting and wheezing, clutching his side. "With time to spare," she announced, nodding like she was impressed. "How'd you manage that?"

"I..." he gulped for air. "Gave them to... Alan." He collapsed into a chair and leaned forward. "I ran into him on the way."

"Good boy," Stacey teased, draping her blouse over his back.

Steve jumped to his feet and pulled Stacey in close, kissing her deeply. He pressed his body hard against hers, and she could feel his already erect cock. His mouth stayed on her lips, her neck, and nibbled her earlobes while she could feel him unclasp his belt and begin working his pants down his legs.

She reached for his shaft and stroked it. Steve moaned into the crook of her neck. He reached behind her and unfastened her bra, slipping it off her shoulders, freeing her breasts for him to massage and kiss. As he played with them, she stroked him faster.

Giving him a gentle shove, Steve took a step back. Stacey reached under her skirt and removed her thong, tossing it on her desk. She walked across the room to the brown leather couch and sat down, sinking back into it with her ass barely on the edge of the seat. She hiked her skirt up and spread her legs wide.

He didn't need further instruction. He kicked his pants to the side and practically dove in front of her.

"Oh yes, right there. Keep at it right there," Stacey instructed calmly, as she began to squirm. "It feels so good..."

Steve was kneeling between her legs. One arm was wrapped around her leg. His other hand was stroking his cock. More importantly, his tongue was pressed directly on her protruding clit, moving around in slow tight circles.

"Mmm, I never get tired of this. Don't stop..." Stacey

moaned words of encouragement to him. Every man needed more than just his dick stroked. Attention must be paid to his ego as well.

The ringing of her cell phone interrupted them. Like a good boy, Steve fetched it. As soon as Stacey answered, he went back to work on her mound. "This is Stacey. Oooh," she said in the phone.

"Sorry. I stubbed my toe. That will not be a problem. Yes. Uhhhhhh. Yes, we can."

She eyed Steve angrily, but he wasn't looking up. "Uh-huh. Just let us know. Oooh. Mmmm."

"Thank yoooouuuuu," she moaned, hanging up.

"You could've shown me the courtesy of pausing," she scolded. "That was important." It was an act. The call was important, but she didn't mind the sexcapades going on during it. She'd flat out scream *fuck my ass harder* while in the middle of a business conference call and not give two shits about doing so.

Steve removed his mouth long enough to say, "You told me not to stop."

It made Stacey grin, and she leaned back again. She grabbed a handful of his hair and pulled his head closer to her box.

When she started writhing against him, growing closer to climax, he inserted a couple fingers and stroked her tunnel to push her over the edge. Her entire body tensed and tightened while the orgasm raked her over then she collapsed. Steve rocked back on his haunches and smiled at her. "My turn," he announced.

The corner of Stacey's mouth lifted into a wry grin. *If he thinks I'm sucking him off after all the flirting he's done with that new hire slut, he's sadly mistaken.'*

She slid forward off the couch until she was on her knees in front of him. Then she turned quickly and bent over the cushions. Steve positioned himself behind her. He brought the tip of his cock to her pussy and pushed inside her. The first full thrust made them both moan. He fucked her slowly at first and steadily increased his speed.

"Oh, yes!" She yelled when he reached around and rubbed her clit. She cried out so loudly the staff on the other side of the door definitely heard her. Not that she cared. In fact, it gave her a brilliant idea.

Stacey batted at his legs for him to move back. He pulled out and waited. Position changes were common with her.

"The desk," she whispered, glancing over her shoulder.

Steve jumped to his feet and extended his hand to help her up.

"I've got an idea." She leaned in and took his bottom lip between her teeth gently.

She walked over the enormous wood desk and leaned all the way over the front of it until she could open a drawer on the other side. She rummaged through it blindly until her fingertips felt what she wanted, and she grabbed it. Steve was already behind her, rubbing her ass cheeks, and ready to continue what they already started.

Stacey spun around before he could position himself to enter her again. He looked surprised. "Here," she said.

He took the bottle from her hands, and a slow smug grin spread across his lips. "Oh, yeah," he moaned lustfully.

She kissed him passionately then bent over the desk, pulling her skirt up to her waist. He stood behind her and carefully kicked her feet apart a little more.

His fingers traced the opening of her ass, and he inserted one finger in to the knuckle. "Are you sure?" he asked.

"I'm always sure."

There was a snap as the lid opened followed by the cool liquid being poured on her. He scooped it up with his fingers as it ran down toward her pussy and smeared it on her ass, inserting his fingers to rub it into her tight walls. She waited patiently while he coated his entire shaft with lube.

The tip of his shaft pressed against her hole, and he pushed forward carefully. "You okay?" he asked.

"Yes." It was almost sweet the way he acted like she was green behind the ears when she was already experienced in how to please a man before he had been born.

His tip disappeared inside her, and he pulled out. He entered her again and pushed harder and deeper. He continued on like this slowly until his entire shaft was buried in her ass.

Stacey moaned loudly to encourage him. He reached a steady rhythm, and she realized he was planning on staying slow and true the whole time like she was delicate. Not for long.

Her hand was a couple inches from her desk phone, and she secretly reached over and pressed the intercom button, keeping it firmly held down to capture every last detail.

"Yes, Steve!" She cried out, happy he couldn't see the devilish look on her face. "Fuck my ass!" She didn't want any of them to wonder about anything.

Steve groaned loudly.

"Harder, Steve," she cried. "Fuck me! Make me yours!"

He pounded into her as hard as he could. His grunts and groans becoming louder. Stacey knocked a few things to the floor to add to the audio show she was performing.

Gasping she cried out, "That's it, Steve! Your cock feels so good. Fuck!"

Steve was close. She could feel his cock pulsating and growing larger.

"Cum in my ass!"

He thrust once more as deep as he could, and she could feel the spray of his cum shoot inside her. He groaned loudly, and she made sure the staff on the other side of the door heard it all.

When he pulled out, she stood up, but kept her finger on the button a little longer. He pulled her to him, holding her from behind, kissing her everywhere.

"You're amazing," she lied.

"You're the best I ever had."

Stacey had no doubts that was the truth. "Who's your girl?" she asked which was out of character for her. It actually made her stomach flip. She could feel the smile form on his lips pressed against her neck.

"You are, baby. I love you."

She let her finger off the intercom button. Ashley better think twice about looking at her toy again. She wasn't the sharing type.

Chapter Seven

The Interview

"*Your company managed to steer through the Me Too movement unscathed.*"

"Yes," Stacey said proudly.

"*It almost doesn't seem possible. How did you accomplish that?*"

"This is probably the biggest difference between the adult entertainment business and every other company. Sex is a daily topic of conversation within Metro Media."

"I make sure all of the new employees are well aware during the interview process of what to expect. Sex will be discussed. Sex toys. Adult films."

"*Yeah, of course. That's the nature of the business.*"

Stacey tried to find the wording she needed. "I think while people know this the average person doesn't realize the extent. They apply for an office job and expect to look at invoices or payroll all day. Or, they apply for the warehouse thinking they'll be unloading boxes off a forklift."

"I make sure they know sex will be discussed at every turn. You will see toys, lubes, condoms, videos daily. They're going to be out. Sometimes you might see an employee handling one for a number of reasons."

She drew a breath and clarified, "Handling, not using." The interviewer laughed along with her.

"They are in the office as well because I like to inspect the new products when they arrive. I make sure they understand this is the environment. It's different than the average job, and it's not for everybody. If they can't handle it, there's no shame in that. I have even allowed trial runs letting them catch up on filing or work on another project to let them make up their mind."

"Right. I bet there are a lot of people who wouldn't be able to do this work."

Stacey ignored the comment. It implied there was something wrong with her line of business. "However, on the flip side of that coin. Just because you're exposed to these products doesn't mean you have to be okay with the rest of it. Employees can inspect toys, hold them, and even turn them on if it vibrates to get an idea of what the product can do. That doesn't give them the right to hold a twelve foot King Kong dong to their groin and waltz around the warehouse hitting co-workers on the ass with a dildo. That is unacceptable, and it will not be tolerated."

"We try our best to maintain a safe space inside this world. Actually, I think we do more to keep it professional here than other companies *because* of the nature of the products we sell. It would be too easy to slip down the rabbit hole. We say on top of it."

"Very good, Stacey. One last question. You've had your own very successful sex toy line for a while now, and I understand you're adding a movie line to it."

Stacey chuckled. "Yes, that is correct."

'What can you tell us about that?'

"The same as my product line, Secret Passions, my new film venture will be geared toward women. It's called Female Desires. The ones in production right now are directed to straight women, but we will be expanding that in the very near future."

"The vast majority of adult films on the market today are aimed at men. There's a huge market being neglected. Men have their own interests. They like cum shots for example. Women don't want to watch a collection of cum shots. For them, it signifies sex is over, and most of them didn't get their climax yet. It's a turn off for a straight woman."

"Women want something with a plot. They don't want a collection of smutty scenes. No poorly written story about fucking the pizza delivery man. It's so overdone. They want something with a little more heart to it. That's what turns women on. These movies will have a better established plot. We're spending more time developing that. We're looking for actors who are not only comfortable fucking on camera, but who can actually hold a scene. It won't be Oscar worthy, but we're trying to meet that market."

"That sounds great. I'm really looking forward to it. I think it will do well. Thank you for taking the time to talk with us today, Stacey."

"No, thank you!"

"We'll be in touch."

The line went dead, and Stacey cradled the handset feeling pleased. The interview went well, and she covered everything she wanted to and more.

"Why do you use the name Maddox?"

Stacey's head jerked up, and she stared at him. She had forgot Steve was in the room sitting on her office couch quietly. Ever since he bent her over the desk without realizing he had an audience, he'd been super clingy. Ashley suddenly and mysteriously lost interest. He quickly figured out Stacey was the only woman in the building who wanted him.

"What do you mean?"

"At the start of the call, you identified yourself as Stacey Maddox, but that's not your name."

"No," Stacey said irritated. "But I was married to the old codger."

"You never took his name. It's something you mentioned a lot. You're always talking about making a name for yourself, but you're using someone else's."

'Oh! This boy did not know who he was dealing with.'

Her extremely busy day was coming to an end, and she didn't have the patience left for this. Stacey inhaled deeply and clasped her fingers together on her desk. "If you must know, you're right. I met him in a business meeting about creating a sex toy line within his company when I was young and idealistic. Not only did he integrate one, but he put me in charge of it."

"When we married, I didn't take his name for a number of reasons. I use it the same way a celebrity might use a stage name. Maddox already has a reputation associated to it in this industry, but my legal name is on all the paperwork."

"The sex party line I incorporated after his death now accounts for over thirty percent of the total business this company does. I also streamlined the video production part of the company cutting our overhead greatly. And, I have my own sex toy line sold by us as well as multiple companies all over the world. The value of this business has more than doubled since I took over."

"So, I have made a name for myself. Would I have been able to do it without his name? Yes, I have no doubt."

She straightened out the paperwork on her desk, tidying up for the day. Steve didn't push it farther, but there were a thousand more thoughts popping into her head like rapid fire. She wanted to scream them all at him. Walking to the door to leave, she added, "Besides I'm the one who had to put up with the impotent kinky fuck long enough to be entitled to a few perks like the recognition his name allows."

Steve didn't push the subject. He fell in step behind her and asked, "Are we going out or back to the house?"

Stacey looked at him blankly.

"It's about quitting time," he said, checking his watch.

"I have other work to do yet, and then I have plans tonight."

"What plans?" he asked. He sounded like a jealous boyfriend which no woman wanted to entertain.

"Plans that don't include you." She waited for the elevator with him. After they stepped inside and pushed the button for the first floor, she walked back out. "Have a good night," she said as the doors closed between them.

She took the stairs and made her way across the building to the warehouse. Everyone had gone home for the day. Near the door was a large U-shaped counter where all the magic happened. She set her purse on it and draped her suit jacket over it.

Hands covered her eyes. "Guess who?"

"Alan," Stacey smiled.

He grabbed her arm and spun her around forcefully. They bumped heads, and one of her arms was pinned in an awkward position against his chest. What the man lacked in grace he made up for in good looks. He was a six foot tall blonde Adonis.

Alan was an odd duck. He was married, but claimed he never cheated even though he had a few regular flings over the years. There were several women, including Stacey, he'd hook up with when the urge hit. His wife always told him if he ever stuck his dick in another woman, she'd cut it off. That's why he uses sex toys on Stacey while beating off and only sticks his dick in the occasional male.

Three minutes later they were naked lying on the floor. Alan was on his back holding a massive eight inch long and obnoxiously thick vibrator on his midsection he held precariously on a small pillow. It always amazed her how he tolerate the discomfort, and probable pain, of this position, but it's the one he chose tonight.

Stacey straddled him with the well lubed tip of the toy teasing the entrance of her tunnel. She lowered her body and eased the tip inside her, already feeling it stretching her walls. This was how he liked it. He picked what, where, and how, but she claimed the when.

She knew he couldn't properly reach behind her to stroke his own very well endowed shaft until she was riding him with the length of the toy buried inside her box. That's why she took it slow when short and fast was her preferred fucking experience. She loved to tease Alan. He has made it clear he dreams of fucking the hell out of her, but he stays true to his wife, in his mind at least.

Raising up, she starts over again. The tip eased in a little farther this time then she repeated the process. Alan's hands were on her hips trying to guide her down the full length, but she fought it. This was going her way or not at all. Eventually, he gave in and allowed her to continue the tease. He should know better by now.

"That's it, my filthy whore," she growled. "You get me on my terms."

The vibrator spread her wide, and she came before she made it to the base. It filled her completely and forced her to comply, opening more to allow it to raid her labyrinth.

She grunted and grinded against it. Alan's face devoured her as he tried to imagine how the eight inches of silicone felt. She grabbed her breasts and rolled her nipples between her fingers.

Alan pulled her upper body down to him, keeping one hand on the base of the vibrator. He did it to keep it in place. If it slid around off the side of his abdomen, it'd ruin their build up. Once he had her in place, he used his free hand to tend to his cock, jacking it against her supple ass cheeks.

Almost every time they hooked up, she thought about it. He was right there exposed and unsuspecting. It wouldn't take much effort to raise up and back capturing his cock between her legs. She wanted it too. It wasn't because of his looks or how good she believed he might be in bed. She wanted him simply because she couldn't have him.

Closing her eyes, she imagined it was Alan's cock plowing into her. She grinded against his hand at the base. The knuckles of his fingers hitting her clit, adding to the sensations bringing her to climax.

His breathing was shallower, and he raised up to her. He kept his mouth inches from her. Kissing was also off the table. This was the most they could ever be.

"Fuck me, Alan!" The fantasy playing in her mind drove the words, but there would be no objection if he took the hint and slammed his pulsating cock in her ass.

He began to jerk and buck, and she felt his sticky load shoot over her lower back and ass. She desperately wanted to feel him cum inside her, in whatever hole he chose.

She quickened her movements, and he gripped her hip, pressing down hard. "That's it, Alan," she moaned. "Make me cum!"

Her body shook from her release, and her juices flowed over his hand. She collapsed onto his chest still hopeful one day she'd have the real thing.

Chapter Eight

Afternoon Delight

Stacey stood up when Steve walked into her home office. "I need your cock," she said as common place as ordering coffee.

He blinked at her in disbelief still holding a small box of files in one hand with a clipboard peering over the top.

She walked up to him and rubbed his crotch through his already tightening jeans. "Follow me," she ordered, leaving the office for the comfort of her bed upstairs. She peeled off her clothing as she went.

"Um, I think Alan needs this paperwork," he said, slowly trailing her.

It was amusing he was actually thinking about his job when his lover was stripping and offering him sex on a silver platter.

Halfway up the stairs, he tried again. "That's why he insisted I bring it over now. I don't want to get in trouble for taking too long."

"Who's your boss?" she asked, disappearing into her bedroom.

Stacey was naked, kneeling on the bed when he finally walked through the doorway. "I was beginning to think you weren't coming," she said with a wink.

"I still have to get the forms signed."

That's when she noticed he was holding the clipboard at his

side. If she wasn't so damn horny, she'd be yelling at him to leave and ripping up his precious paperwork in the process.

His timing had been impeccable, and that was the only reason why she was going to fuck him in her bed in the middle of the afternoon. She'd spent the last hour in a telephone business call while amusing herself online. Before she knew it, she was watching short amateur porn clips and turning herself on. The meeting ended, and she was about to take matters in her own hands when Steve knocked on the door.

"Toss the clipboard down before I fire you," she ordered.

He looked at it then at her before letting it drop to the floor.

"Very good. Now get over here." She patted the bed next to her.

Steve came over and squatted to sit, but a raised eyebrow from her forced him to stop. He kicked off his shoes, tore off his shirt, then yanked down his jeans and boxer briefs in one movement.

Stacey grinned as she watched and licked her lips at the sight of his erect member. "That's it. Sit down."

He did as she requested.

She leaned in and rubbed his shaft with one hand, planting her mouth on his. Her nails gently pinched the skin up his cock as she stroked him. She wasn't looking down, but in her mind, she could see her French tips against his skin. Her nipples were hard and tingling, eagerly awaiting their own attention. They may have to suffer this time around. Her urges were controlling her.

Pressing him back hard, he fell on the bed with his feet on the floor. She moved fast, centering herself over him and lowered herself onto his hard shaft. He tried to sit up to object, wanting more time to play before they got down to the nitty gritty of it. She pushed him back again, covering his mouth with her hand. "Shut up," she commanded.

His eyes twinkled, and he nodded. Then he licked her fingers.

Stacey yanked her hand away from his mouth while he laughed. *'So juvenile.'*

She cradled his head with both hands, grinding on him in slow circles. Her lips gripped his and sucked gently. She lavished attention on his full upper lip, sucking it away from his face, snaking her tongue up behind it.

Her breasts danced against his chest. She rocked back to angle a better position to ride him to orgasm.

Steve reached up with both hands, cupping her breasts. He massaged them gently and pinched her nipples. He tried to lean up to suckle on them, but they were just out of reach. She swatted his hand away when he tried to pull her back to him. Her climax was seconds away, and a changeup could force her to start over, building up to it from scratch.

The muscles in her labyrinth tightened around his shaft. It quivered around his cock as her release flowed down his member. Her movements became stiff, and she tilted her head back letting out a long, drawn out grown. Her body needed this.

After riding out the waves of pleasure, she fell to his chest. He slid her easily to the side and buried his face in her chest. He lapped at her nipples, teasing them with his teeth.

He climbed on top of her, lifting one of her legs over his shoulder, and drove his tip into her tunnel. Then he hovered and slowly moved side to side. "Do you want this cock?" he asked.

'Not anymore,' she thought. Her needs had been satisfied, and

she hated consoling a man's ego in the middle of sex. *'Just fuck me already.'*

Steve asked again. "Do you?"

She told him everything she thought he might want to hear, but she was losing the mood with each lie that came from her mouth. He finally pushed into her box before she was fed up enough to push him off her.

He thrust into her slowly, looking down at where their bodies joined. Their juices and sweat had mixed together into a glistening natural lube, dripping down to the bed. His cock slid into her with no resistance from the aid of her cum, still slowly flowing free.

"Fuck me, Steve," Stacey said softly.

The words were lost on him if he even heard them. He continued one long, deliberate stroke after another. His eyes never wavering from her pussy.

"Steve," she said louder.

This time he lifted his chin and darted his eyes to her face.

"Fuck. Me."

He broke into a wild grin. "Yes, ma'am." He leaned in closer, stretching the leg he positioned next to his head. "You want this?"

Her eyes rolled. She couldn't keep it in. She pressed against his chest to end it right then, but that was the final clue he needed to figure it out. He kept his mouth shut after that, and plowed her pussy.

The raised leg angled her tunnel just enough for him to hit her sweet spot. Her moans were short and high pitched, and she came again in under a minute. Once her body stopped twitching from the strength of her orgasm, he pulled her other leg up on his other shoulder. Her moans increased in tone until her mouth was open, but no sound could be heard. The walls of her labyrinth convulsed around him, showering him in her cum, and the climax didn't end.

Stacey reached the point where she couldn't take anymore, held on and kept going, then reached it again. Something had lit a fire under him. This was the hardest he'd ever fucked her. If he'd been like this from the start, she might have considered him to be more than just her play toy.

"Oh, shit," he mumbled. He pressed his mouth to hers. The rush traveled through his body and out of his hard cock. He thrust hard into her and held himself hard against her body. There were a couple more full thrusts just like it with him holding the ending as long as he could before he collapsed next to her.

It took several minutes for Stacey to catch her breath. She rolled onto her side with her hands under the side of her face and smiled warmly at him. His eyes were still closed, and she waited excitedly for him to look at her.

'What the fuck are you doing?' It was too late for him to be anything but a passing distraction now. She sat up and scooted to the edge of the bed where she grabbed the robe she draped across it that morning.

She stood up and slipped it on. There was a shower in her very near future just as soon as Steve was on his way back to the office.

"Where are you going?" he asked. "Come back. It's almost time for seconds."

Stacey smiled with her back to him. Guys were always the same. Wanting to go harder, longer, setting some kind of sexual records like it proved their ability to provide satisfaction.

"It's time for work," she said, tying the belt of the robe.

"You can't expect me to work now," he moaned.

She picked the clipboard off the floor and walked to the nightstand, fishing through the drawer for a pen. Once she found one, she flipped through the invoices, signing them. "Here," she said, tossing the clipboard on the bed. "Done."

"Seriously, Stace," he begged. His arms outstretched to her, wanting her to lay down with him again.

"Seriously? We both have work to finish, and it wasn't but a few short minutes ago when these papers were oh so important to you." She added the dig about how long it took him to cum to keep him level headed. "And don't call me Stace."

She walked into her bathroom and stood in the hot spray of the water for longer than she had intended to. He would be gone by the time she emerged. They were going to go out tonight, but she'd cancel now. Regardless of the plans they made, there was one, and only one, reason for them to meet up. Those needs had already been fulfilled.

'He was a good guy though,' she thought as she dressed. She had put him through the ringer, but he was still there, by her side, ready for more.

"That doesn't set him apart," she told her closet. She slid hanger after hanger aside, looking for something to wear. "Every man you've ever toyed with was the same way until you grew bored of him and tossed him to the curb."

Stacey wasn't tired of Steve. She was far from it. As mean as she was to him, as hard as she tried to come up with nasty, condescending thoughts about him, there was something different. There was something different about the way she enjoyed his company, and something different about him altogether.

Surely, one of her toys could be promoted to something more. There was a reason she pigeon holed people into select boxes. It made life easier, less messy. *'Was there really anything wrong with doing a little reorganizing?'*

By the time she went back to her home office, she had convinced herself to try it. In the morning, she may change her mind again, but for now, she was entertaining the idea of allowing Steve to become a bit more important to her. She wasn't going to cancel their plans. They'd go out tonight, and she'd treat him decent for a change.

When she picked up her cell phone, she saw he had beat her to the punch anyway. He had ditched her.

The disappointment she felt only lasted about two seconds. It was immediately followed by anger. Not only did he break their date, but he wasn't going to be at work tomorrow either. There was some emergency, and his mommy needed him.

'This is the last time I get duped into thinking a boy could ever do a man's job.'

Stacey vowed to herself she'd be on the prowl tomorrow. After work on Friday, she'd head out and be gone the whole weekend if that's how long it took. She'd not only have her revenge sex on Steve making her feel something again, but she hoped to find a replacement. Steve was out of chances.

When she walked into the office Friday morning, she had no idea how easy it was going to be to do all of the above. The opportunity to put Steve behind her was handed to her on a silver platter by the last person she expected.

"Hold my calls and cancel my appointments." She told

Ashley over the intercom. This was going to require her undivided attention.

Chapter Nine

Angry Sex

He was waiting for her when she arrived that morning, sitting next to her locked office door. His head in his hands. It looked like he'd slept in the hallway. His clothing and hair was so disheveled. When she stood next to him, she could smell the scent of the all in one soap, shampoo, and conditioner body wash he used.

"What's going on, Alan?" she asked. It wasn't out of concern. Stacey didn't appreciate a homeless looking, albeit clean smelling, employee waiting to ambush her first thing in the morning.

Alan slowly pulled himself to his feet but didn't say a word. He pointed to her office door, indicating he wanted to talk in private.

Stacey rolled her eyes with her back to him as she pulled the key from her purse. It had already been a bad morning. Steve was headed back home to his mommy. That boy took days off like he didn't need a job, and that's the position he was going to find himself in on Monday when she fired him. His text this morning informing her he'd be gone all weekend was what she needed to rid herself of thinking he ever had potential to be more with her. With him gone, her weekend plans were shot, and she'd have to go on the prowl to meet her needs.

Now, this? She pushed open the door and walked inside,

hanging her jacket and setting her purse on her desk. *'This isn't going to end well.'* Either he has an emergency and needs time off when the work load in the warehouse is already piled high, or there's a problem with another worker down there.

The door shut behind her, and she took a deep breath. Someone had to be the company bitch, and it always fell on her shoulders. She prepared herself to come out hot, all pistons firing as she tore him a new one about work ethic and responsibility.

Alan grabbed her arm and spun her to face him. Stacey's eyes widened and her mouth fell open to scream, "What the fuck do you think you're doing?"

She never had the chance. He planted his mouth on hers and kissed her so passionately, so deeply, so skillfully. They were moments into the kiss before she entertained the thought this was the first time his lips had ever touched hers.

His hands roamed up her sides, yanking her blouse from her skirt as they traveled until his fingers reached her breasts. He squeezed them hard.

Stacey pulled back. "Alan, what's going on?"

He planted his mouth on hers again.

It was easy to figure out something happened with his wife. Stacey wanted to know the details. She probably left him after finding out the sneaky way he side-stepped her words.

Alan stepped back and stared at her. The look of lust and intent in his eyes excited her. Her already throbbing clit swelled and pulsated with her heartbeat. "Lock the door," Stacey told him.

The office staff were making their way in to their desks. Stacey could hear the voices travel down the hallway. She called Ashley and told her to cancel everything. There was a very important matter which required her undivided attention.

When she cradled the phone, she and Alan charged each other. They met between the chairs near her desk. Hands and mouths were everywhere. Alan ripped her shirt open. The tiny opaque white buttons flew across the room and pinged as they made contact.

Alan took control. He turned Stacey to the chair and fumbled with the zipper on the side of her skirt. When she reached to help him, he pushed her hand away. Once her skirt and thong lay in a heap on the floor at her feet, he gently nudged the back of her knee, and she climbed onto the chair, kneeling and holding the back of it with her hands.

He pushed on her back until she lay over it, and he caressed her ass. He'd smooth his hands over her cheeks, soft and gentle then smack it hard. Stacey yelped in response. He'd grab the already stinging flesh and squeeze. It was driving Stacey crazy. She was realizing she was going to feel this man's cock finally.

"That fucking bitch," he muttered.

It was his wife he was talking about. Whatever she did, Stacey was grateful.

Alan lowered himself behind her and dove into her pussy. He lapped at her lips eagerly, all the while smacking and squeezing her already flaming ass. He sucked her clit into his mouth, angling himself every way he could. Then he raised his head up until his tongue circled her tight ass hole, and he slid one finger, then another in her wet pussy.

This was something Steve refused to do. He'd never eat her ass. Stacey could take it or leave it, but she loved a man who was adventurous. A man who won't eat ass has a long list of acts which are off the table.

The man in her office tongued her hole like he hadn't ate in days. Stacey moaned, saying his name over and over. Each time it rolled off her lips she was reminding herself this was real.

He stood up and pulled her off the chair, half carrying and half dragging her to the couch. Stacey was putty in his hands and would do anything he liked. This was his show today.

The laces on his steel toed shoes were undone, and she realized he must've been working them while eating her snatch. He reached down and pulled his shoes off then dropped his pants. His massive cock swung free in front of her face, and she reached for it. Stacey paused and looked at him to make sure.

"It's yours now," he said angrily.

Stacey wrapped both hands around it and sighed. She stroked it and spit on it to moisten it before wrapping her lips around it. After sliding his full length in her mouth, he grabbed her hair and held her in place. "Fuck yeah!" he yelled.

Alan pulled her head back then repeated it again and again. He let his cock fall out of her mouth and smacked both sides of her face with it. There was so much he was unpacking in a single fuck fest. So much she'd object to under different circumstances.

"Lay down," he told her, stepping away from her. The lustful look returned to his gaze.

She sprawled on the couch with one foot on the floor to give him ample room. "Are you sure?" she asked as he climbed over her.

He didn't answer right away. He positioned his tip and leaned into her like he needed to fill her tunnel with his shaft before either of them had a chance to change their minds. He groaned long and deep as he pushed his full length into her, not pausing to allow her labyrinth to make room for his size.

His full nine inches of thick throbbing meat forced its way inside her, and a shiver coursed through her. It would take seconds for her to climax. Between his size and the pure joy of finally feeling his cock invade her, it brought her to the edge immediately.

He pulled back and slowly entered her again. "That bitch..." he moaned.

Alan's hips moved away from her, and he drove his shaft in a third time. "Fucking..." he spat.

When he shifted to thrust again, he pummeled her pussy. He plowed into her hard, hitting her head against the arm of the couch, moving her whole body until her head was twisted to the side with nowhere else to go. "Cheated on me!" he growled as he pounded her.

This is why she didn't care to keep anyone close to her. Alan had never been faithful. He could play semantics all he wanted, but he probably cheated on his wife more than he slept with her. For him to be fucking her like this, his wife wasn't side-stepping their boundaries. She full on let some other guy ravage her.

Stacey lost track of how many times she came. Her juices ran freely down her legs and puddled under her ass. As soon as she recovered from one, another began to build. She could barely breathe from the workout and the awkward way she was tilted, but she didn't dare say a word. The bliss she felt finally having the one thing which had been denied to her for so long was worth it.

Alan grunted into her, taking all his frustrations out on her pussy. She was happy for it. Angry sex is always an amazing fuck.

He pulled out without warning, and Stacey moaned an almost intelligible, "Nooooo." She had no concept of time. They could've been going at it for hours or minutes. Either way, she wasn't ready for it to end.

"Roll over," he huffed.

Stacey smiled realizing there was more. She did as he asked, and he pushed her up until her ass was on the arm of the couch. Stacey pushed the decorative pieces off the end table but carefully set the plant on the floor. The rug was too expensive for it to break covering everything with dirt.

He crawled up behind her, and Stacey spread as far as she could, welcoming him to take her from behind.

"This might hurt," he said.

Stacey's eyes widened. The lube was in her desk. Her mouth opened, but it was too late.

Alan pushed the head of his cock against her ass and moved forward. It was too tight for him to enter in one stroke, so he pulled out and tried again.

She grabbed the far side of the end table for support and bit her lip till it bled. She'd taken men in her ass dry before but never anyone close to Alan's girth. This was going to hurt, and she was going to love it.

It took close to a dozen attempts before he had a good rhythm going. He moved slowly at first, reaching around to play with her clit. His tempo built slowly until he heard Stacey cry out. The walls of her pussy contracted and vibrated against the walls of her ass he was stretching out. It set him over the top.

He grabbed her shoulders with both hands to keep her still and pounded her ass. "With my own fucking brother!" he screamed.

Stacey heard him, but she couldn't process his words until after it was over. A constant loud moan flew from her throat, growing louder with the increase of his pace. Her ass was going to hurt like hell, and she'd pay for it tomorrow. It didn't matter now. She didn't want Alan to ever quit fucking her like he owned her.

"Fuck! I've wanted this," Alan cried out. He fell forward and shot his hot sticky cum deep into her ass. When he pulled out, Stacey felt it drip out of her.

After they repositioned to sit side by side on the couch, she thought it was going to be a short day. A fucking like that required a shower and some recuperation time. She planned on heading home as soon as he left.

But, he didn't leave.

Minutes later he was hard again and ready for round two. They covered every inch of her office before noon then went back to her house where they didn't see the light of day until they left for work Monday morning. Stacey did the walk of shame to her car. Each step was agony, but she wouldn't have it any other way. Her abdomen to her knees were on fire, and she was looking forward to slinking into her high backed, leather desk chair. Everyone at Metro Media would see she had been properly tended to over the weekend. The dumb fuckers would assume it had been Steve.

'Boy, won't they be surprised,' she smirked, opening the door of her car. *'Steve is going to be out on his ass, and Alan has a hefty promotion announcement even he doesn't know about yet.'*

Chapter Ten

Who's the Boss?

Life couldn't get much better. After a weekend of soul shattering sex, she had a full week of events to look forward too. She and Alan weren't in it for the long haul. Stacey wasn't looking for that with anyone. There had been years of sexual tension building between them. They had done everything but sleep together since before she took over the company. The magnetic draw between them was too great to be satiated over the course of a few days. They would be each other's amusement for quite a while. When the new wears off, she planned on keeping him in her back pocket for whenever the urge might strike. She still wasn't sure what promotion Alan would receive. He already was the warehouse manager, but she'd think of something.

The official launch of her new video line was the next day with the release of the first movie. Her schedule was packed with interviews to promote it. One thing she loved to do was tell the world about her awesomeness and collect their praise.

Getting rid of Steve was the first order of business. She'd been looking forward to it all weekend. The look on his face would be priceless, and she considered recording it.

On the drive to work, she thought about what to do afterward. This week was bringing to conclusion years of hard work. It was all about to pay off. There may be a trip in her future. There were tropical destinations calling her name, and she certainly deserved it.

Stacey pulled into the parking lot early and went to the door. Her alarm code wouldn't work. *'What the hell?'* She tried again with no luck. The third failed attempt would trigger the alarm. She was scrolling through the contacts on her phone looking for their number when the door opened from the inside.

Steve stood there with a goofy grin on his face.

"What the hell are you doing here?"

"I came in early to catch up on some work since I took Friday off."

She glared at him and pushed her way past him. *'I hope he's not expecting to be paid for this extra time when he didn't clear it with me first.'*

"The alarm started acting wonky after I arrived," he said, following her through the hallway. "The company has been called and are sending someone out to fix it."

'Great! Something else to add to my plate today.'

Steve continued to walk with her which was irritating. She liked to have a few minutes to herself in the morning to acclimate to work mode, but it might be better to get this out of the way. It was a shame there'd be no one else here to watch him run out after getting fired.

They got on the elevator, and the doors closed. "I'm glad you're here. There's something I need to discuss with you first thing."

The elevator arrived on the top floor, and they walked to her office door. "Yeah, I got something to go over with you too," Steve said. "If you don't mind, I'd like to go first."

Stacey had a shit eating grin on her face. "Okay."

She put the key in her door, but it wouldn't turn. "That's it!" she screamed. Her face flushed red, and she felt the heat burn her cheeks. "What the fuck is going on?"

Steve pulled a key from his pocket and unlocked the door. He swung it open for her.

"You better start explaining this shit to me right now!"

He extended his arm for her to go in to her own office. "That's what I wanted to talk to you about."

She stormed through the door and found a strange woman sitting at her desk. It was the final straw. She threw her jacket and purse at the woman and exploded in a fit of rage, finally picking up the phone and dialing out.

"What are you doing?" Steve asked.

"I'm calling the police!"

"They've already been called," he said.

Stacey folded her arms over her chest. "Spill it," she spat, glaring at him.

There was a noise behind her. She looked back to see two police officers walk in the room.

"I want these two people to leave immediately. Now! He's fired. If he doesn't leave willingly, escort him off the property. I don't even know who this woman is. I've never seen her before. She's trespassing, and I want her arrested."

No one moved.

She spun around to face the officers. "Aren't you going to do something?"

They looked past her at the woman sitting at the desk. The stranger said, "Give us a moment."

The officers nodded. "Okay, ma'am," one of them said. They took a step back and stood along the wall.

"I wasn't sure if you'd recognize me," the woman said. "We've never met, but I thought you might have seen pictures."

"I don't know who the fuck you are," Stacey said. Her back was still facing the woman. "And quite frankly, I don't give a shit."

The woman said, "Well, you're about to."

Stacey charged at her desk. If the police weren't going to do anything about this, she damn sure would. Right before she reached her, the woman spoke again.

"My name is Marcie Johnson. I'm Steve's mother."

Stacey stopped in her tracks and threw her hands in the air. "Oh, dear God, woman! You have been a thorn in my side since I hired him."

Marcie chuckled. "Yeah? Well, you've been a thorn in mine for a lot longer than that."

"I don't know what the fuck you're talking about, but whatever is going on here, I'm at my limit." Stacey turned to the police once more. "*Please* escort them out of my building."

"You have it all wrong," Marcie said. "They're here to make sure you leave peacefully."

"Me?" Stacey scoffed.

"Yes. This is *my* company."

The words were so preposterous Stacey cackled. The anger inside her had boiled over, and with nowhere else for it to go, it released in the form of wild, maniacal laughter. Her whole body shook from the rage swirling through her. For a moment, she wondered if there was a hidden camera somewhere.

Marcie held up a file folder. "I have the paperwork right here. You signed everything over to me."

"That is the most ridiculous thing I ever heard."

The woman set papers out on the desk in a line. From where she stood, Stacey could recognize her signature. "This doesn't make sense," she muttered.

A memory flashed behind her eyes of a clipboard falling to her bedroom floor. She looked at Steve confused.

He grinned and said, "It looks like she's starting to figure it out mom."

"How could you do this to me?" she asked him.

"Uh, I love my son. Don't get me wrong," Marcie said. "But don't give him that much credit. This was far from his idea."

Stacey looked at her. "So what? Did you just wake up one day and figured the only way you could better your life was if you underhandedly tried to steal someone else's company? You will see me in court for this."

"Gladly. I didn't steal this company any more than you did."

Stacey shook her head. *This can't be happening.*

"William Maddox signed this company over to me," Stacey hissed, slamming her hand on the desk.

Marcie kept her cool. "William Maddox's intent was to temporarily give you control of his company when he was incapable of overseeing it. You're the one who took advantage of his supposed illness, having him sign forms giving you the company outright."

"You don't know what you're talking about." It felt like her entire world was teetering on the edge. She needed to balance it before it crashed around her, but this insufferable woman was making it difficult to think straight.

"Oh, I don't? I was having extensive phone conversations with him at the time. The thing about serious illnesses is they cause people to rethink their actions and make amends. He reached out to me wanting to repair our relationship."

Stacey stared at her like she was speaking a foreign language. There had been no other woman in her husband's life. She was sure of it.

"My married name is Marcie Johnson," the woman grinned, "but I was born Marcie Maddox. William Maddox was my father."

Marcie turned to the police. "It's time. Please escort her out. We've already boxed her things," she said, motioning to the couch. Stacey had been so focused on the two people taking over her office she hadn't noticed them. "I'd like for her to be gone soon. I have a very important meeting in," Marcie said, glancing at her watch, "in about ten minutes regarding the launch of my new movie."

More by Darling Coxx
The Nanny Diaries Series

All five installments of this series are now available! Follow the journey of five young women trying to make their way in the world who have taken jobs as live-in nannies. These books are their diaries. Read about the adventures they had taking care of their own needs. Check them out if you dare! Darling Coxx's writing always scratches the itch you can't reach on your own.

Family Secrets Series

All five installments of this series are now available! Follow five pseudo taboo couplings. They might not be blood related, but they are a little close for some people's comfort. They are pushing the boundaries of what society allows in relationships and enjoying every second they bend the rules.

Supernatural Erotica Series

From vampires and werewolves to witches and ghosts, these books bring an element of paranormal to the bedroom. Every one of these stories is filled with the intrigue and mystery of having a nonhuman lover or at least, a little push from magic to bring their affairs to reality.

Deadly Sins Series

Seven deadly sins; seven highly erotic stories. Each book covers a different deadly sin in the world of sex. It doesn't always work out for the leading lady, or man, but they sure enjoy their trysts while they last.

Spring Break Affairs Series

OH, THE COLLEGE DAYS! What resonates wild sexual abandon more than spring break in another state where there is no one to bring the tales of your conquests back home. Besides, what happens when you're out of state doesn't count, right?

Obeying Orders Series

Do you like being told what to do? Or are you the one who likes being in control? Either way, you'll find someone to relate to in Obeying Orders. Each book is filled with commands to delight every sexual fantasy.

About the Author

Darling Coxx is a seasoned writer who has been featured in many major publications under her given name. Taking a break from interviews and personal experience pieces, she is trying her hand at short novellas in the same genre she's been working in for most of her life.

Her adult entertainment career began while working as the manager of an adult store. It is her favorite position of any she's held, before or since. It was there where she made the contacts that allowed her to venture into the world of adult entertainment both in her own writing as well as producing a few pieces of her own.

Please feel free to reach out to her at DarlingCoxx@gmail.com. Follow her on Instagram @DarlingCoxx to stay updated on future publications.